Max
Goes to the Zoo

by Adria F. Klein
illustrated by Mernie Gallagher-Cole

Special thanks to our advisers for their expertise:

Adria F. Klein, Ph.D.
Professor Emeritus, California State University
San Bernardino, California

Susan Kesselring, M.A., Literacy Educator
Rosemount–Apple Valley–Eagan (Minnesota) School District

Max is going to visit the zoo. He invites his friend Lily.

They want to see all of the animals.

Max and Lily go to see the elephants.

They laugh when an elephant sprays
water on its back.

Max and Lily go to see the polar bears.

They laugh when a polar bear leaps
into a small pond.

Max and Lily go to see the giraffes.

They laugh when a giraffe uses its tongue to grab a leaf.

Max and Lily go to see the monkeys.

They laugh when a monkey uses its tail
to swing from branch to branch.

Max and Lily go to see the lions.

They laugh when a lion cub tries to roar.

Max and Lily go to see the kangaroos.

They laugh when a joey jumps into its mother's pouch.

Max and Lily go to get a treat. They each get a blue snow cone.

They laugh when their tongues
turn blue.

Groundhogs

19

Soon it is time for Max and Lily to go home.

Groundhogs

ZZZZ ZZZZZ

21

Max and Lily had fun at the zoo.

They want to come back soon and see more animals.

WAIT!

DON'T CLOSE THE BOOK!

capstone **kids** .com

THERE'S MORE!

FIND MORE:

Games & Puzzles
Heroes & Villains
Authors & Illustrators

AT...

www.CAPSTONEKIDS.com

STILL WANT MORE?

Find cool websites and more books like this one at www.FACTHOUND.com.
Just type in the BOOK ID: 9781404836778 and you're ready to go!

9